Dear Family and Friends of Young  W9-BEN-574

Learning to read is one of the most important milestones your child will ever attain. Early reading is hard work, but you can make it easier with Hello Readers.

Just like learning to play a sport or an instrument, learning to read requires many opportunities to work on skills. However, you have to get in the game or experience real music to keep interested and motivated. Hello Readers are carefully structured to provide the right level of text for practice and great stories for experiencing the fun of reading.

Try these activities:

• Reading starts with the alphabet, and at the earliest level you may encourage your child to focus on the sounds of letters in words and sounding out words. With more experienced readers, focus on how words are spelled. Be word watchers!

• Go beyond the book—talk about the story, how it compares with other stories and what your child likes about it.

• Comprehension—did your child get it? Have your child retell the story or answer questions you may ask about it.

Another thing children learn to do at this age is learn to ride a bike. You put training wheels on to help them in the beginning and guide the bike from behind. Hello Readers help you support your child and then you get to watch them take off as skilled readers.

—Francie Alexander
Chief Academic Officer,
Scholastic Education

To Amelia, Jeremy, and Bennett
—E.B.

To Thomas & Matthew
—T.P.

ISBN 0-439-44152-8

Text copyright © 2002 by Elizabeth Bennett.
Illustrations copyright © 2002 by Thomas Payne.
All rights reserved. Published by Scholastic Inc.

SCHOLASTIC and HELLO READER! and associated logos
are trademarks and/or registered trademarks of Scholastic Inc.

12 11 10 9 8 7 6 5 4 3 2   2 3 4 5 6 7/0

Printed in the U.S.A.
First printing, November 2002

The Biggest Snowman Ever!

by Elizabeth Bennett
Illustrated by Thomas Payne

Hello Reader! — Level 1

SCHOLASTIC INC.

New York   Toronto   London   Auckland   Sydney
Mexico City   New Delhi   Hong Kong   Buenos Aires

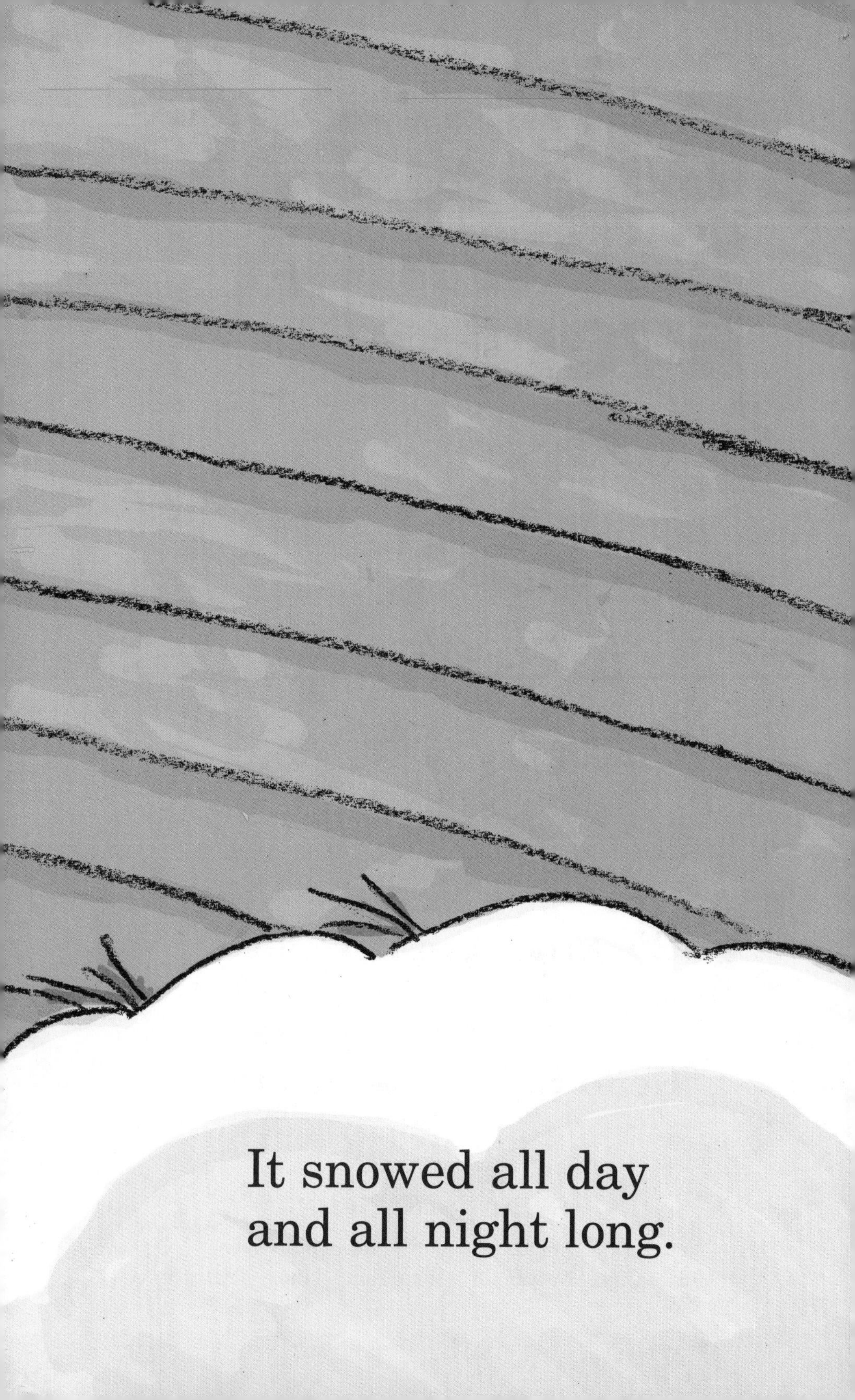

It snowed all day
and all night long.

I'll make a snowman.
He'll be big and strong.

My brothers say
that I'm too small.

They do not want
my help at all.

I make a ball
out of the snow.

I roll and watch it
grow and grow.

Oh, no!

Again, I try to make a ball.
My snowman will be
very tall.

I roll and watch it
grow and grow.

Oh, no!

One last time, I pack
the snow.

I roll and watch it
grow and grow.

Oh, no!

Hey! Wait a minute!
I made a snowman.

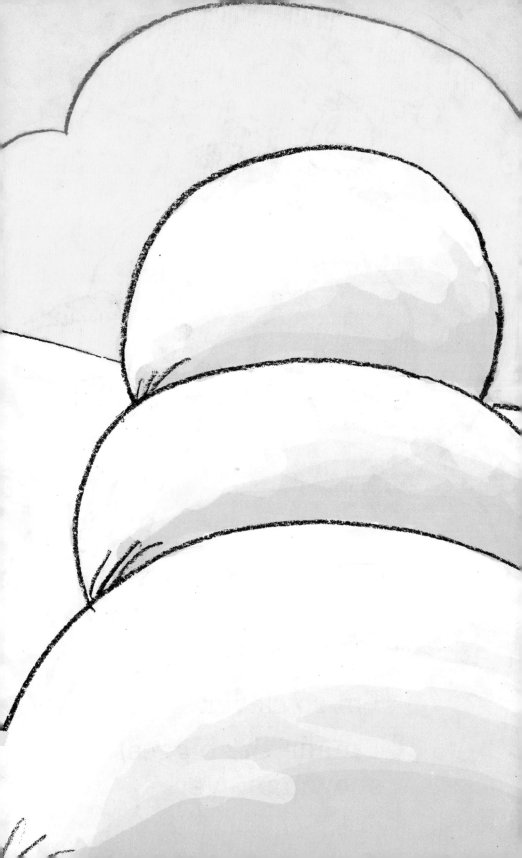

I'm so clever.
I made the biggest
snowman ever!